FACE THE MUSIC

FACE THE MUSIC

Lesley Choyce

orca soundings

ORCA BOOK PUBLISHERS

Published in Canada and the United States in 2022 by Orca Book Publishers.
orcabook.com

Library and Archives Canada Cataloguing in Publication
Title: Face the music / Lesley Choyce.
Names: Choyce, Lesley, 1951- author.
Series: Orca soundings.
Description: Series statement: Orca soundings
Identifiers: Canadiana (print) 20210164573 | Canadiana (ebook) 20210164603 |
ISBN 9781459832886 (softcover) | ISBN 9781459832893 (PDF) | ISBN 9781459832909 (EPUB)
Classification: LCC PS8555.H668 F33 2022 | DDC jC813/.54—dc23

Library of Congress Control Number: 2021934059

Summary: In this high-interest accessible novel for teen readers, Tyler and his friend Mason are desperate to escape the small town they've grown up in.

Orca Book Publishers is committed to reducing the consumption of nonrenewable resources in the production of our books. We make every effort to use materials that support a sustainable future.

Orca Book Publishers gratefully acknowledges the support for its publishing programs provided by the following agencies: the Government of Canada, the Canada Council for the Arts and the Province of British Columbia through the BC Arts Council and the Book Publishing Tax Credit.

Design by Ella Collier
Edited by Tanya Trafford
Cover photography by Getty Images/Mehmet Şeşen (front) and Shutterstock.com/Krasovski Dmitri (back)

Printed and bound in Canada.

25 24 23 22 • 1 2 3 4

For Kelty MacGregor

Chapter One

Mason and I had been talking about leaving for a long time. But that's all it was. Just talk. And it was mostly him doing the talking. Finally, though, he convinced me to do it. Get up early, real early, while it was still dark. Steal a car from a driveway down the street. He said he knew of a guy who always left his key in his beat-up Honda Civic. It would be easy. We'd be out of here and gone.

So one day we just did it. It actually was as easy as that. We didn't even pack anything. I did whatever Mason told me to do. I met him at the street corner at 4:00 a.m. We walked up to the driveway and got into the car. He showed me the key that was under the floor mat, stuck it in the ignition and started it right up. Then we backed out of the driveway and headed down the road. Just like that. It felt like a dream.

But it all went downhill from there.

Mason was so confident about stealing that old beater that I didn't even question him. But he forgot one important thing—making sure it had enough gas in the tank to get us to the city.

Did I mention that the sun wasn't up yet? It was still dark when the car conked out on the highway. "Maybe we should forget about it," I told Mason. "Let's hitchhike back home and hope we can get a ride before anyone even knows we're gone. Let's leave the damn car. Nobody will even know it was us that stole it."

"Don't be stupid. We've been talking about this for a long time. You want to crawl back home with our tails between our legs?"

"I just have a bad feeling about this," I said.

"Don't be a shit. If you want to go home, go. We got this far and I'm sticking with the plan. I'm done with all those assholes back there. And I'm not going back home to take more crap from my father."

It was true. We both hated that town. And although my father wasn't as mean as Mason's, he'd been on my case ever since I could remember.

But here we were, stuck in a stolen car on the side of the road in the dark. We had absolutely no plan for what to do next.

Chapter Two

It wasn't the first time I'd followed Mason into trouble. But it was the worst. And stupidest. I had always trusted him, and I didn't know why. Maybe because he was like an older brother to me, and sometimes he could play that role well. He'd been out of school for a year now, even though he hadn't graduated. I still had a year to go. When the last day before summer vacation came around, I really was happy to walk out the door. And I wasn't sure I wanted to go back. I hated school, so why bother?

I knew my parents would fight me the whole way about not graduating. I didn't exactly have a happy home life. Sure, it was a bit better than Mason's, but not by much. My mother and father fought a lot. They were so different from each other and seemed to disagree about everything. My mom had never moved more than a mile away from where she'd grown up. My father had been born here too, but he was the son of an immigrant—my crazy grandfather didn't speak a word of English. My dad grew up with kids making fun of his accent, even though he did his best to cover up anything about his family or past. His advice to me was always "Keep your head down. Don't cause trouble or bring attention to yourself. And don't screw up your life."

He shouted a lot when he said stuff like that to me, but he never hit me. Not like Mason's old fart of a father. But I definitely didn't want to have to face either of my parents about quitting school. And I sure wasn't going to tell them I was leaving this town for good. With Mason.

Mason had convinced me it would be easy enough to steal that car and make a run for it. Down the highway to the city and then maybe beyond. As we sat there in the dark car, I had to admit that, scary as this whole thing was, I didn't want to go back.

"Let's just leave the car then. Let's walk," I said.

He didn't like that suggestion. In fact, he usually didn't much like anything I said. "I'm the ideas man, Tyler," he said. "We need our own set of wheels and that's that."

Which was bullshit. Because here we were, at the very beginning of the big escape that was supposed to go off without a hitch. But the car was dead. And like an idiot, Mason kept grinding away at the ignition. "Look, man," I said, "we're out of gas. The car isn't going to start." He kept cranking away anyway until the battery went dead. Then he slammed a fist into the steering wheel like it was the car's fault.

"What now?" I asked.

Mason turned to me, a sneer on his face. "This wouldn't have happened if I had been on my own. I'd have been gone long ago. But it took so frigging long to convince you. So I waited it out. And now look where we are."

I knew how Mason's mind worked. He liked to blame me for whatever screwed-up thing happened to us. And there were a lot of screwed-up things in our history. I knew this wasn't my fault, except for the part where I'd just followed him blindly, believing he knew what he was doing. I could have said a lot of things right then. But I kept my damn mouth shut.

Chapter Three

Just when I thought we were totally screwed, it got worse. Mason got out of the car and started kicking at the door. He'd always had a bad temper and a nasty habit of bashing at things that made him mad. And he got mad a lot.

He screamed out loud. Once. Twice. Three times. I kept telling him to get back in the car so we could think this through.

"No, you idiot! You get out of the car!" Mason shouted.

And I should have gotten out of the car right then and started walking back home. If I was lucky, I could get back before anyone even knew I was gone. But Mason was acting like a maniac. I didn't trust him. He was sure to start taking his anger out on me. So I reached over and locked the driver's door. Then my door.

This infuriated him. "Get out of the damn car, Tyler," he snarled. But I sat tight.

And then Mason did that thing, that reversal he did in every damn jam we'd ever gotten ourselves into.

He laughed.

He put his mug up to the car window and made a goofy face. "Shit," he said, the anger seeping out of him. "We're finally on our way, dude."

"Barely," I said. "Just barely."

"So the car's dead. So what?" He had done his classic about-face. The whole bloody fiasco was now a joke. "Come on. Let's walk. Let's torch the car. Just watch it burn."

"No. Don't be stupid."

And he would do it too. He'd pull that lighter out of his pocket and set the car on fire. So I did the only thing I could. I opened my door and got out. I walked around to his side of the car. Sure enough, right then he took out his lighter and flicked it on. The flame lit up his face, making him look like...what? A ghost? A devil?

"Put that away," I insisted. "All it will do is attract attention. Bring cops."

He flicked the lighter closed. "Guess you're right. Let's get out of here." And then Mason just shrugged.

So we started walking. It was cold, and we weren't dressed for the weather. What was the plan now? Neither of us said a word. Right then I wanted to be anywhere but here. With anyone but him.

I didn't know what was going through his mind, only that he was looking for someone to blame, and out here there was only me. I was the only one to pin it on. "You really fucked this up, Tyler. You really did it this time."

"How did I fuck it up? You were the one who didn't check the gas."

"I waited for you, buddy. I've been waiting for months. I waited until you were ready to leave. I would have left a long time ago. But I hung in there for you."

This wasn't exactly true. We'd talked about leaving, but it was Mason who'd always talked us out of it. I think deep down he was scared to do it on his own and needed me as a sidekick. Or at least needed someone to blame if anything went wrong. And now it had.

I stopped in my tracks. Now I was the one who was angry. Boiling angry. I was finally tired of taking crap from him. Mason walked a few feet ahead and then stopped and turned around. "What's wrong with you?" he said in that nasty-ass voice he used when he wanted to intimidate people. And that sent me over the line.

I threw myself at the bastard and tackled him. He was caught totally off guard as I dragged him to the ground.

When I had him pinned, he looked up at me and growled like a wild animal. But I had him down and was about to smash him good, something I'd never done before. Not like this anyway. The look on his face was pure hatred.

That's when I heard a car approaching. It was slowing down behind us, and we were caught in its headlights. I didn't care. I had the creep pinned, and in a second, I would have smashed him good. Behind me I heard the car come to a stop. Someone got out. Before I could even turn to see what was going on, someone grabbed me from behind and pulled me off Mason. At first I could only get a glimpse of him—a big hulking guy with long straggly hair, powerful arms and a crazed look in his eyes. He threw me to the ground.

Chapter Four

The guy tried to help Mason up, but Mason lashed out at him. The barrel-chested hulk roared something I couldn't quite make out, grabbed Mason by the shoulders and threw him down on the ground beside me. Then he just stood there in the headlights, his jaw clenched, his hands curled into fists. "Who the hell are you two little shits anyway? And what are you doing, trying to kill each other here by the side of the frigging road?"

It looked like he was ready to go at us again, so we both lay there frozen on the ground. Mason looked at me. His anger toward me was gone. Did we now have a new common danger, a new enemy? Whoever this guy was, he clearly looked like a wild man—the angry, violent, crazy type. Some escaped murderer out driving in the dark, looking for his next victims? A lunatic ready to kill for the thrill of it?

Instead he said, "Now what am I going to do with you?"

"Just fuck off, asshole," Mason shot back. "Leave us alone."

The guy still looked threatening, and the glare of the headlights made him look even more like a madman.

"I should do just that," he said as he turned and started to walk back to his car. The engine was still running. It had that low rumble that a real muscle machine makes.

"Wait," I said. "Give us a ride." I was feeling desperate now. Shaken. "Please."

He stopped, paused, then turned and walked back to us. "Did you just say please?"

I nodded. For once Mason kept his mouth shut.

The next thing we knew, the guy was sitting down on the ground beside us and breathing hard.

Mason looked like he was ready to run, but I gave him a hand signal to stay put. I tried to study this big brute with long hair who might still, at any minute, decide to beat the crap out of both of us, if not outright murder us. He was looking right at me when it suddenly struck me that he seemed familiar. I couldn't quite place where, but I'd seen him before. And then it clicked. "Aren't you—?" I began.

"Oh, here we go," he said. "Don't start that shit."

"Dakota, right? Sean Dakota."

"Dead wrong," he said. "Never heard of him."

Now Mason was standing up. And a smile spread over his face. He was looking right at him. "Holy shit. You are him. Freaking Sean Dakota. Man, I've seen all your videos. I can't believe it's you. Wait until I tell people about this."

I didn't know who he thought he was going to tell.

That stopped the guy dead in his tracks. "Now I'm gonna have to kill ya," he said, reaching into his pocket for something.

Was he joking? Or was he serious? There was no way to tell. As his hand slid out of his pocket, I was expecting to see a knife. Instead he curled his hand into a fist.

"We won't tell a soul," I said, suddenly remembering that Sean Dakota had been reported missing from his California home and that no one had seen him in close to a year. Most people assumed he was dead. But here he was, by the side of the highway in our neck of the woods. Suspicious and ready to protect his whereabouts, even if he had to kill us. I noticed the multiple tattoos on both of his very muscular arms and the strange one on his neck.

"I'm gonna get back in my car and drive down the road," he said through gritted teeth. "And I don't want you mentioning you've seen me to anyone." He had his fist up in the air now—clearly a threat.

I swallowed hard, but Mason just glared back at him.

"Both of you keep your mouths shut and don't tell anyone I'm anywhere around here. I like being lost. I love that no one can find me and I intend to keep it that way. You got it?"

"Okay," I said. "Sure."

But Mason couldn't keep his mouth shut. "Man, I don't know how you're going to do that. You're pretty hard to miss. Almost anyone could recognize you."

Sean stood there for a long couple of seconds. "In town I make a point of looking different, okay? Got some straight-ass clothes. Short-hair wig. Glasses." He was holding his hand out now to help Mason up. "Before I split, though, tell me something. What the hell are you two up to out here so goddamned early?"

"We were running away," Mason said. "What's that to you?"

Something about Sean suddenly changed. "Running away from what?"

"Same old shit," Mason said. "Crappy life in a crappy town."

"Running away? Really?"

"Really," Mason said.

Sean now looked strangely puzzled about something. He'd lost the tough-guy thing he'd had going on before. "Get up," he told me.

I stood up and brushed myself off.

"Everybody should run away at least once," Sean said.

It was not at all what I had expected him to say, but I thought I should try to keep the weird conversation going. "Why is that?" I asked.

"Because it's a cruel, nasty, unfair, uncaring world out there. And the best you can do in this shit life is get the hell away from all the rats and the bloodsuckers."

"That why you're here instead of California?" I asked.

"Something like that," he said. He studied us some more and then let out kind of a snort. "You little shits don't know the half of it, do you?"

Chapter Five

No, we probably didn't know much about how bad things could get. All we knew was that we were fed up with our lives back home.

Now Sean walked toward me and came so close I could smell the stink of his sweat and his putrid breath landing on me. He shoved his face up close to mine, but I couldn't look him in the eye. He had that crazed look in him again like I'd only seen on actors in movies—the bad guys, the killers. "Look at this, stumphead," he said.

I stared at his thick neck. He had a totally weird tattoo of an old-style vacuum cleaner. What the hell?

"You recognize that?" he asked.

I had no idea what he was talking about.

But then Mason was standing beside me. He was looking the guy in the eye. "No shit?" he said after studying the monster's neck.

"No shit," the guy repeated.

"Your first band," Mason said.

Sean smiled. "Ancient history. But it was the real thing. Real music. Before I went solo and sold out to those fuckers." He gave a kind of snort with a bit of snot flying out of his nostrils. Some of the anger was coming back now. "Just remember, you tell anyone I'm here, and I chop off whatever part of your anatomy you treasure most."

I looked at the tattoo again and shot a questioning look at Mason.

"I still don't believe it," Mason said. "I thought you were dead."

"Everyone thinks I'm dead. And that's the way I like it."

"And that's why you're here," I added.

"Boy genius," he said.

I didn't want to say the wrong thing. Or even the right thing. I still wasn't in on the secret. I gave Mason another questioning look.

"Vacuum Head," Mason informed me, explaining the tattoo. "His first band. I used to listen to them. All the time. In their day, Vacuum Head was one of the best death metal bands in the country."

"Close but no cigar, dipweed. It wasn't death metal. It was grindcore. There's a serious difference to the discerning fan. And we weren't the best in the country. We were the best in the world."

"Until you made your exit," Mason said.

"You got that part of the story correct, shit-for-brains."

It suddenly registered on my radar. Not that I paid all that much attention to the kind of angry, loud music that Mason seemed to love more than any other. But it had been on the news and all over the internet about this guy, Sean Dakota, just walking off the stage in the middle of a big concert in Los Angeles. And then no one hearing from him again. There was a lot of speculation that he had offed himself, since suicide was in the lyrics of so many of his songs. Apparently, there were no clues as to where he'd gone and what had happened to him beyond that. Just gone. Presumed dead.

Sean took a deep breath. "So seriously, lads, if you're running away, why are you here and not far, far away?"

"We ran out of gas," I said as Mason shot me another evil look.

Sean laughed a demented laugh. "The Boy Scout motto is Be Prepared," he said. "Guess you punks were never in Scouts."

"I guess not," I said.

"And I suppose that, given the hour of the day, no one knows you're gone?"

"Nope," Mason said.

"So I could just waste both of you and no one would be the wiser?"

"Yup," Mason said again like an idiot. Me, I was thinking this former rock-star legend was crazy enough to off us if he wanted. I gave Mason a kick in the shins. He deserved a lot more.

Sean must have seen the look on my face. "Don't worry, dipweed, I wouldn't waste the energy. I just don't know what to do with you two. You're the only two people in the world who know where I am. I was pretty happy all on my own." He paused. "Well, maybe not happy. But at least I wasn't having to put up with whiners and ass-kissers." He paused again, looked up at the sky and just shook his head. Then he let out a big sigh.

"Okay. Get in my car," Sean Dakota said. "I'll drive you to the city and drop you off somewhere. You better keep your mouths shut."

I wasn't sure abut this guy anymore. I didn't quite trust him. But Mason nodded. "Fantastic," he said. Maybe he thought it would be cool driving somewhere with such a famous guy. I did my usual. I followed Mason's lead.

Mason sat in the front seat and I got in the back, alongside a beat-up acoustic guitar. Sean popped the clutch and squealed his tires as he pulled back onto the road. There were a few awkward moments of silence until Mason asked the obvious question. "I know you say you were unhappy. But how could you do it? Why walk away from the fans, the music, the money, the fun?"

"Fun?" Sean said, looking straight ahead. "The fun had gone out of it a long time before that. I'm not sure it ever was fun. Maybe at the beginning. With Vacuum Head. Playing an old Gibson electric plugged into a 30-watt amp in my cousin's garage. After that it became nonstop late nights, endless days on the road with my bandmates farting in the bus. Shitty people. Shitty deals. Bad dope. Bad decisions. Bad lifestyle. I couldn't even sleep properly anymore. So I closed up shop. It just hit me like a shot of lightning right there onstage."

"And here you are," I said, trying to get into the discussion.

I realized now there was a bit of light outside. The sun was coming up behind us in the east. Sean cracked a smile. "Just another day in paradise." Sean did this funny thing then. He lifted his hands off the wheel entirely and drove with his elbows. "What about you two turkeys? Most of us have gripes against Mommy and Daddy back home. But what's so bad that it sends you fleeing from your roost in the middle of the frigging night?"

Mason looked like he didn't want to answer, so I gave Sean the short version. "School sucks. Everybody in town kept saying I'd turn out like my father. He could never keep a job or make a go of it. He always pissed everyone off. Made my life hell too. I had to get out."

"He hit you?"

"No. Well, not any time recently."

"Then what did you have to complain about?"

I decided not to answer, since I didn't have a smart comeback. But the question must have loosened Mason's tongue, because he piped up. "My father liked to whack me around. I took it until I couldn't take it anymore. Sometimes you just have to get away, ya know?"

Sean turned on the overhead light. He was studying the tip of his little finger now. "Got any scars to prove it?" he asked.

"What?" Mason snapped back.

"Scars? Like these?" Sean lunged toward Mason, made a fist and stuck his right arm in Mason's face. He had scars, all right. Knife cuts, it looked like, up and down his arm—some even looked like they had tattoos created around them. "Mom wasn't too interested in raising her boy, but Pop thought a little pain would toughen me up for the real world. The music saved me. But then it went bad too."

"I'm sorry to hear that," I said. For such a big, rough character, this Sean Dakota seemed oddly likable to me now that he wasn't trying to kill us.

He put his hands back on the wheel and reached for a travel mug of something. He took a sip. "I used to say I liked my women the way I like my coffee—strong and bitter." He paused. "But that was all bullshit too. At first my whole hard, angry-boy routine felt like the real thing. But the more I played it up for the fans, the more I didn't like it. I didn't like *me*. So one day I just buggered off."

Now, staring straight ahead, Sean's expression changed. "You know, I have no idea why I stopped when I saw you guys fighting. I go for a lot of all-night drives to be alone on the road with my thoughts. I make a point of not getting involved in anyone's life, anyone's situation. And now I have you two turds in my car. Maybe I should have offed both of you. No one would ever know."

Sean ran his fingers through his long shaggy hair. "But I guess I won't bother," he added. "Well, then, if I'm not gonna kill you, what *am* I going to do with you? Any suggestions?"

"Just give us that ride to the city," I said. "We won't tell anyone about you. They wouldn't believe us anyway."

Chapter Six

The whole murder routine wasn't for real. I knew that now. It was silent in the car for a long stretch. In the light of the early dawn, I noticed a bunch of drawings in the back seat. Some crazy, scary scrawled artwork. "You do these?" I asked, holding them up for Sean to see in the rearview mirror.

"Yeah," he said. "Helps me express my inner demons."

"I can see that. You have talent."

He shrugged. "I have nightmares."

"Sometimes it amounts to the same thing."

He nodded and graced me with that devil-tinged smile. Looking in the mirror again, he asked, "Okay, smart guy, what do you do for fun when you're not running away from Mommy and Daddy?"

I didn't really have an answer. Fun wasn't part of my regular routine back home. But Mason had an answer. "We steal things."

"Theft—the world's oldest profession," Sean said.

I had heard otherwise but decided not to comment.

"I guess I stole things as a kid too," Sean said. "Never thought much about it. But then once I had some money and stuff, people started stealing from me. I didn't like it."

"Friends shouldn't steal from friends," I said, but I realized Mason was right. We did steal things. We stole for the hell of it. We stole for fun and had done it on many occasions. Mostly money from unlocked houses. Mostly from people that Mason claimed "deserved it."

"Where'd you learn that?" Sean asked. "Sunday school?"

"Something like that," I said. "But now look where it got us. Stuck on the side of the road in a dead car."

"What doesn't kill you—" Sean began.

"Makes you stronger," Mason finished.

"No. I was going to say what doesn't kill you makes you avoid doing it again. The Bible according to Sean Dakota."

"You should write a book," Mason said sarcastically. Another thing Mason did for fun was insult people—even people he liked. I wished he'd just keep his mouth shut.

Sean suddenly jerked the car off the road. We were in front of someone's house. "I'm going for a walk over to that bush there and take a piss. If you two thumbsuckers are gone when I come back, I might not exactly celebrate, but I'd sure appreciate it."

Sean opened the door and got out. He left the keys in the ignition and the car running.

Once he was gone, Mason turned around and gave me a look. I didn't like it. I knew what Mason was thinking. "No way," I said. "God damn it. Don't even think about it."

I could tell Mason was ready to make his move. Just slide over and drive us off. But he hesitated. And then Sean was back. "Shrubbery's watered, boys," he said.

"I had a thought," he said as he got back in the car. "I think I should take you two numbskulls back to your home. You're a liability to me, and I can see that you both will just fuck it up when you get to the city. I know your type. I never signed on to be a babysitter for a couple of dimwit punks. What say you go home and face the music?"

"We're not going back," Mason insisted. Then he suddenly lifted his shirt so Sean could see the burn marks on his chest. Burns his father had given him as a kid. "The bruises have long since healed," Mason said, "but dear ol' dad gave me these souvenirs to remind me that he was the one in charge."

Sean sat there staring at Mason until he lowered his shirt.

"Okay," Sean said. "I get it now. I'll take you both where you want to go. You can figure out something from there."

Chapter Seven

The sun was fully up now, and things got quiet again in the car as we drove into downtown. Sean put on a pair of nerdy-looking sunglasses and one of those caps like you see old Irish guys wearing. He pulled into a fast-food drive-through and got himself another coffee but didn't ask us if we wanted any. Before he pulled back out into traffic, he said, "Now you've succeeded at running away," he said. "So what's your plan?"

The truth is, we never had a plan. I had blindly followed Mason's incompetent lead and only by luck had we gotten this far.

Sean could read that on our faces. "I should just leave you two dimwits from Nowhereville right here. You think you're ready to take on the world, but you don't have enough brain cells to survive a single day."

That pretty much summed it up.

"Okay, okay," he said, exasperated. "I got a shithole of a crash pad up the street. You can stay a couple of days until you get your bearings. Then you get out of my life. And don't tell anyone about me or how I saved your sorry selves. It would totally wreck my image."

If he had dropped out of the spotlight of the metal music world, I wondered, why would he care about his image? Regardless, we owed him big-time.

"Okay, man," Mason said. "That would be great."

"Yeah, thanks," I said. "Thanks again."

Sean's apartment was bigger than I'd expected. It was on the second floor of an old industrial building that had been converted into apartments. But Sean's place looked like someone had started to renovate it and then given up. The walls were unfinished. There were piles of books everywhere. Amps were stacked against a wall, and microphone stands were in a jumble as if someone had done battle with them. Their cords were tangled and stretched out across the floor in all directions. Several electric guitars leaned against what little furniture there was. The place was a disaster. But it was warm, and we were inside.

Sean pointed to a room that had a single metal bed. It had no windows and looked like it had once been a storage room. "There," he said. "It ain't the Hilton, and we don't have no frigging room service.

Stay there, get yourselves organized. I want you two shitheads out of here in two days max." And as an afterthought, he added, "No, you can't drink the beer in the fridge, and don't eat my food. And stay the hell out of my way."

Chapter Eight

Sean tossed a key to the floor in front of us. He had changed into what he called his "businessman dirtball outfit," topped off with the nerdy glasses and a really bad short-hair wig. Then he just walked out the door like he had some important business to attend to. Mason looked at me as he picked up the key. "Well, we're here. We made it. I told you it would all turn out okay."

Nothing had turned out anything like Mason had said it would. But whatever. We were in the city and had escaped the hole we grew up in. Now it was time to get to know our new surroundings.

I guess we both were feeling pretty good as we walked out of Sean's apartment and onto the street. I was surprised at how busy the city was. Mason was checking out the girls and saying rude things, but I wasn't paying him much attention. I was just taking it all in. I'd been here a few times but never on my own. I had never walked around like this, looking at stuff.

So we really were here. Now what?

We turned down an even busier street. I spotted a number of people sitting on the sidewalk, asking for change. We passed a couple of old geezers holding out coffee cups. They mumbled at us when we didn't contribute. Then there were two teens, a girl with long braided hair, sitting with a German shepherd, and another skinny, punk-looking kid holding a sign that read *Need Money To Get Back Home.* I would have stopped to talk to them, but Mason kept moving. He seemed to be looking for something, studying what was happening on the street.

On one corner, across from a park, we came across a guy in a suit and tie, playing classical music on a violin. Not toe-tapping fiddle music but the serious-sounding stuff. In front of him was a violin case. The bills and coins looked like they'd add up to at least fifty dollars. Mason froze right there in front of the musician. He was staring right at the money in the case when someone leaned forward from the small crowd that had gathered. He dropped a fiver into the case.

Mason looked at me and smiled.

"No way," I said.

But Mason had already made his move. He elbowed a couple of people who had stopped to listen and lunged at the violin case full of cash. He grabbed it, flipped it shut and ran right out into the street. He dodged cars, slamming his fist down on the hood of a truck that nearly ran him over.

I should have just stood there and done nothing or walked slowly away in the opposite direction. But I'd been going along with Mason's lead on things for so long, my instinct was to run and follow him. So I did.

I was only slightly more cautious than Mason as I worked my way along the crowded sidewalk and out onto the street. Cars honked at me. I made it across and through the iron gate of the park. I saw Mason over by the fountain. I'd always been a faster runner than he was, so it didn't take me too long to catch him.

He stopped when I got close. We were standing beside a dirty pond with a bunch of ducks swimming around. Mason was breathing hard but smiling. "Did you see how easy that was?" he asked.

"Did you see how many people were watching?" I fired back.

He set the violin case on the ground and opened it. He started stuffing the bills and coins into his pockets. Then he took a handful of coins and shoved them at me. I just looked at him.

"C'mon, Tyler. Free money, fool. Take it."

So I jammed one fistful of coins into my pants pocket and then another. When the case was empty, Mason tossed it into the muddy water. Scared, the ducks flapped their wings across the pond and took off into the sky.

Mason looked quite proud of himself. "Let's get out of here," he said. We started walking toward the gate at the opposite end of the park.

I should have known by now that going along with Mason was never a good idea. He had led me into trouble plenty of times before. But I had always looked up to him. He was older, smarter—or so I thought. A guy willing to stick his neck out and take some chances. And he had been my ticket out of our hometown and a dead-end life.

But we were a couple of kids from out of town who didn't know how fast things could move in the city. We were caught totally off guard when two policemen stopped us as we stepped out of the park onto the sidewalk. Somebody had reported us. We were probably the easiest criminals to track down in the history of the police department.

They had seen us heading out of the park and cornered us as soon as we went through the gate. Each of us was grabbed by an officer. They said nothing.

Mason piped up first. His usual denial of guilt and claim of innocence. "We didn't do anything! What is this?"

The cop holding Mason slapped a pair of handcuffs around his wrists, held on to them with one hand and shoved a cell phone in Mason's face. I wasn't putting up any struggle and was spared the cuffs. I could see the little screen from where I stood. Someone had videoed Mason's entire already-famous heist and sent it to the police. Things really did move fast in the city. Damn.

Chapter Nine

I can't say the police were overly nasty to us, but they weren't exactly nice. Everything about them seemed to say, *We're just doing our job.* Without any further conversation, we were put in the back of a police car and driven to the station. There we had to hand over the stolen cash. A woman in uniform counted it. "Fifty-seven dollars and change," she said.

She opened our wallets and wrote down our names and addresses from our ID cards. And we just sat there on some hard wooden benches for a really long time while they ignored us and went about their work. I thought about trying to explain that I myself hadn't done anything. I wasn't the thief. But even if I could convince them of that, I'd feel like I was abandoning my old friend. So I didn't say anything. We sat in silence until the uniformed woman came in and said, "We checked up on you with the police back in your town. They seem to think you two boys are trouble. They also said they had a report of a stolen car. Someone saw a couple of guys matching your description stealing it. You wouldn't happen to know where the owner can get his car back, would you?"

I didn't say a word, but almost immediately Mason piped up. "Not a chance."

She was a little surprised at his answer. "I see," she said. And I wondered why Mason had been stupid enough to be snarky and put us in deeper shit than we were already in.

We were led to a jail cell in the basement of the building. Most of the cells were empty except for a few drunks sleeping it off. We were put in the same cell. It was straight out of something we'd seen on TV, only now we were living it instead of watching it.

Once again I was starting to feel angry at Mason. He had gotten us into this. I would have never been so bold or so stupid as to steal from the busker in front of that crowd of people. Or be caught on video by some tourist filming the musician. I started to lay into him, but he put his fist in front of my face. "Just shut up, Tyler. Just shut the fuck up."

And so we spent our first night ever in a lockup. Mason cursed out loud in his sleep and jumped up once screaming. I guess he didn't remember where he was. By 2:00 a.m. I was starting to wish I was back home in my own imperfect household, sleeping in my own bed.

In the morning we were taken upstairs, and the same cop said we could be released if we promised to appear for a court date. She handed us some paperwork and looked at me. "But because you're still sixteen, Tyler, we will need someone to come and collect you. Do you want to call your parents?"

"No," I answered. "Definitely not."

"But I'm free to go?" Mason asked.

What the hell? So clearly *he* was ready to abandon *me*, if given the opportunity.

She looked us over and answered, "No. You're in this together. I decide when you both leave. Where are you staying?"

I had made a mental note of the address of Sean's apartment. "At 2012 Brunswick Street. Apartment 12."

"Will someone there vouch for you?" she asked.

"Yes, of course," Mason said. He was such a bullshitter that his reflexes kicked in as soon as she asked the question.

"Got a name for this person?"

"Sean Dakota," he answered, already failing to keep his bargain with Sean. I watched her reaction. The name didn't ring any bells.

"Phone number?"

Mason raised his hands in a shrug.

"Okay. We'll send someone over there."

As she picked up the phone, Mason looked my way. He didn't have to ask the question out loud. *Would Sean Dakota come bail us out?* If he had said it out loud, I would have replied, *Not in a million years.*

"You want to wait here or go back to your bunks?"

"Right here will be just fine," I answered, expecting it could be a mighty long wait and wondering what they would do with us when Sean didn't show up.

But an hour later, there he was. He still had the monkey suit and sunglasses on but no wig. He spotted us as soon as he walked in. He spoke with the cop. It was a fairly lengthy discussion. He took off his sunglasses as he signed some paperwork. Then he walked our way. He didn't say a word.

At that moment a young policeman entered the room and looked over at us. He took a long look at Sean. He leaned over a desk to speak to the woman who'd been keeping an eye on us. He asked her something, and she pointed to the document Sean had signed. He walked over to us.

"Sean Dakota?" he asked.

Sean looked around nervously, then nodded.

"I thought you had gone missing," the cop said.

"I was just on vacation," he replied.

"They said you were dead," the cop added.

"Well, clearly they were mistaken."

"Can I get your autograph?"

"Sure," Sean said and signed the little notepad the cop held out. "Let's go, boys," he said to us.

We obediently stood up and followed him out of the police station into a rainy morning in the city.

Chapter Ten

There were a lot of cops in the police-station parking lot. Sean kept clenching and unclenching his fists and was breathing kind of funny. Sean was the kind of guy who couldn't hide his real feelings, I guess. We were without a doubt a couple of stupid losers—busted our first day in the city. Two of the cops, drinking coffee from paper cups, stared at us as we made our way to Sean's car.

“Get in,” Sean said, giving a dirty look to the two staring cops. They just kept staring. He didn’t like that. “Better go find some donuts, boys!” he yelled over to them. He was a real charmer.

Mason tried to get in the front again, but Sean stopped him. “In the back, scumbag,” he said. So we both plunked down in the back seat. Sean planted himself behind the wheel and turned around to look at us. “I have no words to express how I’m feeling right now.” But I could tell from the look of him that he was steaming mad. “And now you’ve blown my cover as well.”

I had already noticed that Sean liked to pose most anything he said to us in the form of an insult or a threat. He had obviously honed this skill during his time on the road as front man for Vacuum Head. He made a move to start the car, but then turned around again and screamed at us at the top of his lungs. “How stupid can you be?”

It was what my high-school English teacher used to call a rhetorical question, meaning that it didn't require an answer. But leave it to Mason to offer what he thought was a reasonable explanation. "The money was just there for the taking," he said with a shrug.

Sean raised his fist in that now-familiar manner and screamed in Mason's face, "You don't steal from musicians, asshole!" Droplets of spit sprayed over us.

This outburst drew the attention of the two coffee cops, who now ambled over our way. The larger one tapped on Sean's window, and he slowly rolled it down.

"Problem here?" the cop asked.

Sean sucked back some snot and ran his hand through his long dirty hair. "Just trying to impart a bit of hard-won wisdom to the lads," he said in a voice borrowed from a British sitcom.

The cop ducked his head lower and half leaned into the window to look at us. "Oh, Jesus. Those two." He looked back at Sean. "Good luck," he said.

"Thank you, officer," Sean said, still using his mock accent. The cops sauntered off, shaking their heads.

Sean ran both hands once around the steering wheel and leaned back, half turning toward us. "You already have a rep now as the two dumbest thieves in the history of the city. And here I am, seen sitting in a car with you. I don't know why I'm doing this."

I suppose I should have kept my mouth shut, but there was a big question in my head. I blurted it out. "Why *are* you doing this?"

He stared at the windshield, caressed the steering wheel some more and then turned the key. The car groaned and sputtered before the ignition caught and the engine started with a rumble. "Because I was once a young asshole like you two."

We drove back to Sean's apartment and he cooked us some scrambled eggs while listening to some outrageously loud and angry music by a girl band he claimed was "the best in the business." The eggs were good. Sean's mood was oddly cheerful.

"I decided I'm gonna pull together a new band," he said. "Record some tracks I have in my head. Go back on the road. The hermit stint was good for a while. But it's not me. I miss the stink of the crowd. I miss the noise and the nightlife. I miss the music."

He rambled on for a while about the music and about his plans to show himself in public and get back on the stage. "They'll say I'm back from the dead. I like that. I can work with that."

"Go for it, man," Mason said. "Can we be roadies or something?"

I had no idea what a roadie's life would be like. Hauling gear, I supposed. Hanging out backstage.

Late nights in sketchy bars with sketchy people. Was that really what I wanted? Hell yeah.

"In a word, no." Sean shot that down quick enough.

And then the phone rang. Not a cell phone. Sean didn't seem to use a cell phone. This was an old-style land-line phone, hanging on the wall. Sean let it ring, like, eight times. He looked at it, though, as if looking at it would make it stop ringing. "No one ever calls me unless it's bad news. No one really even knows I'm here. Ignore it."

But on about the thirteenth ring, he gave in. He killed the music and picked it up. "Yo."

All we could here was his end of the conversation. "What?...Shit...Why are you calling me now?...You're lying...You what?...What are they saying?...You want me...there?...After all the crap you put me through?...No way...No...Fuck it." And he hung up.

Sean was back in angry mode. It was his default status for a lot of the time, it seemed. But now he looked angrier than usual. Neither Mason nor I asked what the phone call was about. Suddenly Sean picked up his plate with the scrambled eggs and ketchup on it and threw it down on the floor. The plate shattered, and eggs and ketchup splattered the wall.

"That was my father," he said. "He's out in California. He says he's dying. He wants me to come see him."

"I thought you hated your father," Mason said. We'd heard a few of Sean's family stories in our short time together, as each of us had tried to prove we'd had it worse than the others. But Sean had won every time.

"I do. Or at least I did. But he's calling me and asking me to be there for him. He sounded so weak. And helpless." The anger had gone with the smashed plate. Here was someone—just another human being—about to lose a parent. The guy was a bundle of contradictions.

He walked over to a kitchen drawer, opened it, took out what looked like a rolled-up wad of money and shoved it into a pocket. He leaned over the sink to splash water in his face. "I gotta go," he said. "You two punks can stay a couple of days to get your shit together. And then leave the key with the super downstairs. Don't let me find you here when I get back."

And then he was gone. Just like that.

Since we'd left home there'd never been a dull moment. But something about that phone call and the way Sean had changed right in front of me made me feel funny. Homesick almost. I thought about my own parents and how they must be wondering what had become of me. I had wanted to say something to Sean about his father. Ask him if there was anything we could do to help. But I didn't know what to say, so I kept quiet.

Now he was gone and we'd probably never see him again. We just kept bouncing from one bad thing to the next. I wanted to go back. Go home.

But as I was about to admit all of this to Mason, I saw that big smile flash on his face.

Chapter Eleven

Sean had only been gone about ten minutes when Mason opened that kitchen drawer and started rooting around. He pulled out a small wallet and lifted out six credit cards. "Bingo," he said.

"Put them back," I said.

But then he found an envelope, and his eyes lit up. He opened it and dumped the contents on the kitchen table. Money. Lots of it. Twenties and fifties. I'd never ever even seen a fifty-dollar bill before. "The jackpot," Mason said. There must have been a thousand dollars there.

"It's not ours, Mason," I insisted.

"It is now."

"Mason, you can't be serious. Sean has been good to us. He brought us here, let us stay in his home. He freaking got us out of jail. And it was your stupidity that put us there. Don't do this."

Mason just looked at me and shook his head. Then he laughed and started scooping up the bills from the table. "I *am* doing this. We take the money and we split." He was looking around the apartment now, and I realized he was checking to see what else he could steal.

"He took us in. The guy's father is dying, and now you're stealing his cash and credit cards? You can't be serious."

"Looking out for number one," he answered. He held up the envelope of cash. "With this we can go somewhere else. We can have some fun."

"And then what?"

"Who cares? This is just plain old good luck."

"It's not luck, Mason. It's stealing from a guy who was kind to us."

Mason shook his head. "It's Sean Dakota. He's got plenty more. It won't matter if he loses a little."

"It'll matter to me. Don't do this."

"What are you saying? You're not with me on this?"

"Hell no. I'm *definitely* not with you." I have no idea where my nerve came from, but I was not following Mason this time.

"Fine. Then I guess I'm on my own. I was going to split it with you."

"I'm not letting you take it!" I was yelling at him now. I was really pissed.

"Try stopping me."

I'd had enough. I lunged at him where he stood, knocking over a chair. I pushed him to the floor. All my life I'd been following Mason's lead. He was always enlisting me in one scheme or another. He was always telling me how things were so stacked against guys like us that we had a right to fight back any way we could.

But now it was finally sinking in. Mason was a greedy bastard who didn't care what he did to anyone if he thought it was good for him.

The money spilled onto the floor. I had Mason on his back now and was pinning him down. I saw the rage on his face. I was so damn mad at him that I just held him there, locking down both of his hands. If I moved, he'd be up and pounding me, so I kept pressing down, the full weight of me on top of him.

He roared, and his eyes blazed. When he made his move, I knew I wouldn't be able to keep him down. I knew full well that he was stronger than me. And even before he pushed me off him, I realized things could never be the same between us. I knew that whatever happened next, Mason and I were no longer friends.

But it was worse than that. He roared again, pushed up with all his might and sent me spilling backward into the fallen chair, which jammed into my back. And then he was on top of me, pinning me this time. Only he had me held down with one hand on my throat, choking me. I couldn't breathe. I watched as he raised his other hand and made it into a fist. I hoped it was a threat, that he would stop there. If I moved ever so slightly, the hand on my neck gripped tighter. I tried to tell him to let go. I wanted to say, *I give up*. But I couldn't even squeeze the words out.

And that fist just hung there, with Mason leering down at me like he hated me more than all the people he thought had done him wrong in life.

And then the fist came down hard on my face. On my jaw once. Then my nose. My eye. The side of my head. And then things went black.

Chapter Twelve

When I woke up, I ached all over but especially in my head. I had blood all over my face, my left eye was swollen almost shut, and there was ringing in my ear. Mason was gone. The money was gone from the floor. I lay there stunned. I'd been in fights before. But not like this. And it was Mason who had done the beating. After all we'd been through. He'd turned on me because I didn't want him to steal from Sean. The hard and nasty truth was sinking in deep.

The next hour, sitting alone in Sean's apartment, pain throbbing in my eye and in my skull, I guess you could say I had an awakening. I finally grabbed on to the fallen chair and stood up awkwardly. I had pain in my chest and stomach now as well. Had he continued to beat on me like I was a punching bag even after I had passed out? It was all too much to think about.

I walked into the bathroom, hobbling all the way. I looked at my face in the mirror. The puffy red eye, the blood. I washed it off and stared at my damaged mug again, then spoke out loud. "You stupid idiot," I said. "You dumb turd." Yeah, I needed to scold myself for being so blind that I'd let Mason coach me in all the wrong directions ever since we were kids. For a split second I wondered if he would come back and apologize. I don't know why that thought went through my head. But I swished it away. Even if he did, I wouldn't follow his lead ever again.

Time to get on with my own life, I was thinking. Maybe I was realizing this for the first time in my life. I'd always been a follower. Too weak to make my own decisions. Looking to escape from an unhappy family, a bad time at school, avoiding other kids who made fun of me. I'd let Mason be my protector, but he'd used that role to make me do bad things. Cruel things.

But that was behind me. Everything would be different from now on. I was on my own. Really on my own.

The next five days changed my life.

What did I do?

For the most part, I sat alone in the apartment and thought.

I know that sounds crazy. But I'd never really

been alone before. Never sat quietly for hours with just my own thoughts. Probably almost no one but a real hermit ever does that. You sit there with no phone, no TV, no video games, no internet—like we used to say, "no nothing." You face yourself. And in my case, that meant owning up to who I was and what I'd done. I was a follower, not a leader. Mason had been my captain. I was weak. I'd done what he told me to do. What Mason thought was cool, I'd thought was cool. What he wanted, I'd wanted.

But now this.

The pain in my head slowly faded away. I had some bruises on my stomach and my face. My eye was still puffy, but my vision was okay. I drank Sean's coffee. I ate some canned soups I found in his kitchen cupboards and a couple of packages of hot dogs from his freezer. I didn't know how long it would be before he came back, but I'd decided I had to stay, however long it took. I'd tell him about Mason stealing his credit cards and money, and

I'd tell him that I would try to pay him back. Maybe he'd blame me, and maybe I'd get yet another beating. I'd already seen Sean's temper. But I was determined to stay.

No phone calls. No word from Sean. No Mason showing up at the door to apologize to me.

On the sixth day I went out for a walk. I retraced our steps from our first day in the city until I reached the guy in the suit playing classical music on the street near the park. I stood back and listened to the sweet sound of the violin. I guess he'd found a new case somehow. There were only a handful of coins in there. Pedestrians were carving a path around him and not really paying much attention.

After a while he noticed me. Maybe he even recognized me from the day he was ripped off. He nodded and changed what he was playing. Not classical now, but a haunting, familiar folk tune of some sort. What was it? I finally recognized it as an old traditional song that had sometimes been played at funerals I'd been to. I closed my eyes and drifted back to the funeral of my grandfather when I was five years old. And suddenly I was that little boy again. Crying, yes. But my parents were beside me, holding my hands.

When the music stopped, I opened my eyes. The violinist lowered his bow and fiddle. He motioned for me to come toward him, and I inched forward.

"I thought you needed that," he said in a soft voice.

"The song?"

"Yes. I recognized you."

"I wasn't the one who stole your money."

"I know. But I saw you follow that other boy, and I could read the whole scenario. I even thought about you afterward and somehow knew your story. I mean, not the whole story, but the basics. I study people every day, all day. I have gotten pretty good at it."

I wasn't sure I knew what he was talking about. Maybe he was just another crazy man—a crazy old dude who played the violin on street corners. But he certainly didn't scare me.

"It's not like I'm a mind reader or anything," he said, now sipping probably cold coffee from a paper cup. "I could see you weren't one of the city kids from around here. So I guessed you were new in town. I could see you were the sidekick of that swift-footed thief but figured maybe you two were really down and out and needed the money to eat."

"It wasn't exactly like that," I said.

"But close?" he added. "What happened after that?"

"We got busted."

"Ouch. Sorry to hear that. And then?"

I told him about Sean, about the bigger theft. "And now I'm on my own," I said.

"'If you are lonely when you are alone, you are in bad company.'"

"What?"

"Sorry. It's a quote. I've always liked it," he said.

"Actually, it's not so bad being alone. At least right now. It feels good."

"Then the quote is apt. Maybe you're not really alone. Perhaps you are in good company."

"I'd like to pay you back for what Mason stole."

"Well, that would be much appreciated, thank you."

"Only problem is I don't have it now."

"Well, I kind of knew that too. So you can pay it back sometime later. To me or someone else. Doesn't matter. It will amount to the same. You got a name?"

"Tyler."

"I'm Jacob, Tyler. Nice to meet you. Used to play in an orchestra, if you can believe it. Then kind of fell down on my luck. And here I am."

"Sorry to hear that."

"Don't be sorry. I rather like what I do, most days. You should try to find the thing you were meant to do. Something you can feel good about."

I think I felt a chill just then. I knew that what he said was kind of a preachy do-gooder thing to say, but it rang true. All my life I hadn't felt good about much of anything I'd done. I'd followed Mason or done whatever was in my head to avoid getting caught or avoid being singled out or... avoid being me.

Jacob took another sip of his coffee and set the cup back down on the sidewalk. He picked up his violin and pulled the bow effortlessly across the strings in one long, somber note, then slid into that song again. He nodded, and I turned and walked back to Sean's apartment.

When I got there I did the damnedest thing. I cleaned the place from top to bottom. I organized Sean's CD collection, fixed a couple of broken shelves and a loose hanging door. I scrubbed the bathtub and the toilet. And later that night fell into a deep, deep sleep.

Chapter Thirteen

I had to decide whether to stay on at Sean's and wait for his return or leave and try to make it on my own in the city. It occurred to me more than once that the best thing might be to simply make my way back home and return to my old life. School wouldn't start until September, and although I had previously decided not to go back, I didn't really see a better alternative.

But I had no way of contacting Sean to try to explain about Mason and the stolen money. And I had a court appearance that I would have to face soon. Mason wouldn't show, I knew that. But I wasn't going to skip out on one more thing. The more I thought about it, the surer I was that I needed to stay on, explain to Sean what had happened and face the music, as he had put it.

I went looking for work in hopes of earning a few dollars so I could at least take care of myself and attempt to pay Jacob back. Maybe even start to pay back Sean. I tried several supermarkets to see if there was something they'd hire me to do–stock shelves or return shopping carts–but had no luck. I went into the public library and searched online for something–anything–but had no luck there either, even though I found the library the most friendly and comfortable place in the city. Beyond its doors, however, everything seemed alien to me. I just didn't fit in anywhere. I tried looking for work at some car repair shops and convenience stores, but whoever I spoke to took one look at me and shook their head. It was really depressing.

Then one day Sean returned. He just walked in, looking rumpled and discouraged. When he saw me sitting on the sofa, reading one of his books, he took a deep breath and ran a hand through his hair. "Why are you still here?"

I explained about Mason—the cash, the credit cards, the fight. Sean listened and didn't say anything. The story didn't seem to surprise him at all. He sat down at the kitchen table and looked around. I think he noticed I had cleaned the place. A puzzled look came over his face, but he didn't say anything about that either. He picked up a salt shaker and gripped it tightly in his hand, like he was trying to crush it. "He died," he finally said. "My father. Before he died, he told me things about himself I never knew. He said he was sorry for being a crap parent.

Said he made mistakes. Over the years he'd tried to get in touch with me, to talk, to try to patch things up. But I always ignored him or pushed him away. I was still running. Running away from him, from home, from me. I was wrong about running away. Once you start, you just keep running. You never stop."

"I'm sorry for your loss," I said, an expression I'd heard many times before when someone back home had died. It was a good one for when you didn't know what to say.

"I was with him when he died. He was holding my hand. He was still telling me he was sorry. How he wished he'd been able to tell me that sooner. It was so stupid of me to ignore him all those years. And now he's gone."

A heavy silence hung over the room after that. I didn't know what to say. Sean sat there looking gloomy. And then suddenly he threw the salt shaker at the wall. It shattered. He walked toward me. "Get up," he said.

I stood up.

"I want to be alone. You have to leave."

I nodded. I understood. "I'm going to pay you back for what Mason stole," I said. I meant it, even though I didn't have a clue how I was going to do that.

"I don't care about the money. Just go."

So I left. I didn't see that I had any choice.

I was in a bit of a daze as I walked toward the door. I set his key on the table. Once outside, I felt more alone than I'd ever felt in my life. I thought maybe I should have just followed Mason's lead as always. Taken the money and run. At least I wouldn't be so alone. I'd stayed to explain things to Sean, to try to accept some responsibility for the trouble I'd gotten into with Mason. But now this.

I didn't have it in me to face more rejection looking for work. So just like that I became one of those scruffy kids you see on the street. I panhandled for change from strangers. But I wasn't good at it. And I hated doing it. By the end of my first day on the street, I had succeeded in getting only six dollars in change. I wandered toward the harbor and started looking for someplace to crash for the night.

The search took me to an abandoned warehouse with broken windows and pigeons flapping around in the rafters. I found an old sleeping bag left there by some previous refugee, and, despite its smell, I tucked myself into it. The pigeons kept me awake. I hadn't realized pigeons could be so noisy. The damp wind blew in through the broken windows and made some eerie sounds. There were other noises as well. Scratching, a kind of rustling sound, and I didn't know what it was. I tried not to think about it until a rat ran right over my face. I couldn't see it, but it must have been a big rat, the kind they say come in on ships from across the ocean. It scared the piss out of me. So I sat upright, stiff as a board, my back up against the cold concrete wall. I stared into the darkness and couldn't fall back asleep. I sat frozen like that with the smelly sleeping bag wrapped around me, listening to the damn rats scurrying around the warehouse until the thin gray light of morning greeted me.

I was cold and I was hungry and I'd just spent the worst night of my life, alone and scared in the city. Anything would be better than this. I thought about Mason again. Should I have followed him one more time? Taken his lead and headed off farther down the road from home? It definitely would have been better than this. I wrestled myself out of the sleeping bag and tossed it away. It was covered in pigeon shit. I'd had enough of rats and pigeons.

I walked out of that hellhole and into the morning sun just as it was burning through the fog above the harbor. I could see the bridge across the water, and it seemed to be levitating, the fog beneath it on either shore. It was just floating there above the mist. But I started walking in the opposite direction. No plan really. I didn't have the heart to beg for change. So I just let my feet guide me.

Soon I was back near the park, and I heard the familiar sound of Jacob's violin. I followed it as it grew louder until I stood in the small group of people that had gathered this morning. Jacob didn't see me at first as I studied the faces of those around me. They were all well-dressed men and women. I assumed they were on their way to work and had stopped briefly to take in Jacob's performance. A couple dropped coins and bills into his violin case. As I listened intently to each note issuing perfectly from the violin, I suddenly realized I wanted to be like one of them. I wanted to be ordinary. I wanted to fit in. All my life I'd been fighting against a life where it seemed everyone was against me. Most of that wasn't my fault. But Mason had convinced me it was a mean world out there and I needed to fight for what I wanted. Fight. Cheat. Lie. Steal. Whatever it took.

And that's what had ultimately led me to where I'd been the previous night.

Jacob was in a kind of trance as he played, but as he finished playing one tune, leaving the note to linger and fade in the morning air, he opened his eyes. He looked my way and nodded, put his bow back onto the strings and played the familiar opening notes of that funeral song. I realized I had at least one friend in the world.

Some of the audience moved on, and a few other pedestrians stopped to listen. More people headed to work. More individuals with those ordinary lives. I was sure I'd never be one of them.

That's when I saw him. Sean Dakota had stopped to listen to Jacob play his serious tunes. He, too, had his eyes closed. He was unshaven, and his hair was wild. In the old ratty coat he was wearing, he looked like the stereotypical bum I imagined I would be someday. He stood like that until the tune ended, and then he moved forward and dropped a couple of twenties into Jacob's case. Jacob nodded, and I could see from his face that this wasn't the first time Sean had come by.

When Sean turned to leave, he spotted me. He paused, and I was sure he was going to just turn and walk away. Instead he walked toward me.

At first he just stood there and shook his head. I expected him to say something mean. "You look like shit," he finally said.

"I know."

"And you smell like shit."

"I know," I repeated.

Jacob had returned to playing—a classical piece—but people were mostly just walking by now. Sean nodded toward the violinist. "This guy is the real thing," he said. "It was guys like that who made me think once that music could save me. Save me from myself."

"And did it?" I asked.

"For a while. But then I lost it. It wasn't the music anymore. It was the money. The hype. The fame. So I quit. But I was wrong in doing that."

I didn't know what to say, so I said nothing.

"My point is, I was wrong about a lot of things. I was wrong to cut myself off from my father, the only parent I ever knew. I was wrong to abandon my band. They were a bunch of crazy screw-ups, but they were loyal."

"Maybe you can get back together," I offered, not thinking. Who was I to give advice?

"Nah. That door closed. They moved on. I gotta move on too." He turned his attention back to Jacob and the music, and I thought maybe that was the end of it. But instead he continued. "But you, you're different. You still got a shot at things."

"I think I've screwed up every opportunity I ever had."

"You probably did. But that doesn't mean you have to keep doing it."

"I let Mason go. The only friend I ever had."

"No, kid. You were smart to let that asshole run off. I just wish you could have stopped him from stealing my money."

"Sorry, man."

"I learned early on that a truly bad friend is worse than having no friend at all. And trust me, that dude was bad." Sean looked up at the sky, and then he turned back and looked me straight in the eye.

I wasn't sure what to say.

"Well," Sean said. It sounded like he was ending the conversation and was about to walk away. "Well, I woke up this morning and started thinking that I should move on to some other place. I've been spotted here now. Thanks to you and your friend.

And because I was getting sloppy and lazy about lying low. But then I started thinking about you."

"Me?"

"You, you little weasel. That's why I came down here. I came looking for you."

"Why?"

"Because I'm going to take you back to that place you once called home."

"I can't go home," I said.

"Why not?" he asked, his face inches away from mine.

The dude still could be scary when he wanted to be.

Chapter Fourteen

Sean invited me back to his apartment, where I took a shower and put on some of his clothes. They were too big for me but smelled way better. I watched him pack a backpack and take an acoustic guitar off the wall and put it into a case. Outside, the sun was bright and the sky was blue. There was no wind at all, and the harbor was like a mirror below us as we crossed over the bridge. We headed east in his big muscle car.

"What am I going to tell them?" I asked.

"Who?"

"My parents."

"Tell them you're home. Tell them you took a vacation."

"My father's going to go through the roof."

"Face the music, buddy. Face the music."

"But everyone back there will know I screwed up yet again. Stole a car, ditched it, went to the city, got arrested."

"Yep. You did all that and then some. Suck it up."

It wasn't exactly brilliant advice, but there it was. I'd made my move. I'd done the thing Mason and I had always talked about. Leaving home, leaving everything behind and starting over. But it hadn't turned out as I had hoped. Now I was going home. To face the music.

It was late in the afternoon by the time we turned off the highway into the town where I had lived my entire life. I pointed out the run-down, weathered house I had grown up in. Sean pulled onto the patchy grass in the front yard. "Go in," he said. "I'm going to sit right here in the car and listen for all hell to break loose. If it gets real bad you can come and get me. Otherwise..." His voice trailed off, and he gave me a smug look.

"Right," I said. "Face the music. Suck it up. Any other brilliant advice?"

"Yes, soldier. Just do it."

So I did it.

My father screamed, called me every bad thing he could think of. I stayed calm and admitted I'd made a mistake, said that I was sorry. My mother just stood there, scowling at me, and watched as my father ranted about how he'd known for a long time I'd never amount to anything and how he'd been right about that.

I squeezed out a couple more apologies, but they didn't seem to matter. I waited for him to smack me like Mason's dad would have done. It didn't happen though. After what felt like hours of this, it was like he just ran out of steam. He went to the refrigerator, took out a bottle of beer and sat down at the kitchen table. As he sipped from it, he stared at the label.

I walked back out to see if Sean was still there. He was. He was sitting in the back seat of his car, strumming some chords on the acoustic guitar. "How'd it go?" he asked.

"Mostly as I expected," I said.

"And?" he asked.

"My mother says she wants you to come in for dinner."

Chapter Fifteen

By the time we sat down to eat, I was starving. Once Sean came into the house, my father didn't say another mean word to me. He glared at me once or twice, but that was it. My mother was acting the way she always did when we had company over. She apologized for everything. The messy house, the way she was dressed, the food on the table.

Sean just nodded and said things like, "This is great." And "I wish I had a mother like you."

All through the meal, my father rattled on about how business was bad and how few customers he'd had at the garage lately. He stared at Sean's arms and admired the tattoos. This prompted Sean to remove his shirt and show off more of the scary body art. "You should see what's on my ass," he joked. (Or at least I think he was joking.)

There was more talk about music and cars. Once we'd finished eating, Sean took my father outside and lifted up the hood of his car so he could admire the engine. My father was impressed, and Sean said he'd let him drive it if he wanted to. They kept talking well into the evening. My dad took him into the living room to show him his collection of early rock-and-roll records. It was about the weirdest homecoming anyone could imagine.

I helped my mom clean up the dishes without her asking. And that made her cry. "You've changed," she said.

"I'm trying," I said. I wanted to say more, but I thought I might start crying too.

I slept in my bed that night and did a lot of thinking about what to do with my life. Now that Mason wasn't around to lead me in all the wrong directions. It wasn't easy. It was like I didn't know who I was.

It had been too late to drive back to the city, so Sean slept in his car, even though my dad offered him the sofa. Sean said, "I love sleeping in the car. It makes me feel like a teenager again." In the morning he looked like shit, but when he came in for a cup of coffee he said, "I feel like a new man. Must be the air out here. I should quit the damn rat race in the city and move out here."

I thought he was joking, but my dad didn't.

"My brother has a fixer-upper he'd rent ya. I could get it for ya cheap."

"Deal," Sean said. "But I may piss off the neighbors. I was thinking of getting a few of the boys back together to record some new tunes. It could be loud."

My dad just laughed and hit him on the back like they were old buddies. "This ol' town could use some shaking up."

And shake the place up is just what he did.

No one could believe that Sean Dakota had moved into a run-down old place in our town. It attracted some pretty strange fans, but Sean discouraged them from coming around by throwing rocks at their cars when they showed up. He was that kind of guy.

Sean told my father he could borrow his car whenever he wanted. My father did just that, and, if you can believe it, sometimes my father asked me to go for rides with him just for fun. He claimed that people seeing him in that car improved his business at the garage immensely. He said it was the first decent piece of luck he'd had in a long, long time. And we started acting more like father and son than we ever had before.

Sean built a recording studio in the basement of his house, and his bandmates came out and stayed for days at a time. His bass player, Dirty Ike, gave me an old electric Fender bass and taught me how to play. He insisted I practice until the tips of my fingers bled. It hurt like hell, but I stuck with it. Eventually I developed calluses and could follow a tune.

When my court date came up, Sean drove me to the city. We picked up Jacob, who told the judge I wasn't the one who had stolen the money. I owned up to being an accessory to the crime and also took some responsibility for the theft of the car. But no charges had been laid, so that wasn't really an issue. I was given what they call a slap on the wrist. A warning. But a warning fair and square.

I swore I'd do anything to keep from having to sleep beneath pigeon crap with rats crawling over my face ever again.

Without Mason, I had to learn how to make all my own decisions. That was scary at first, but I got the hang of it. When Sean and his band told me they were getting ready to hit the road for a cross-country tour in September, I said I wanted to go along as a roadie. He told me to fuck off.

"September, dipweed," he added, putting me into what I now knew to be a friendly headlock. "September means school. School is crap, but you need to finish. Keep practicing on that bass and talk to me when you're done school. You never know where the road will take you."

One morning at the end of August, a big converted bus pulled up. I helped the band pack up the amps and gear. And then Sean was gone.

I wondered if I would ever see him again. I kept track of him on the internet, of course. The music, the interviews with the rowdy, raunchy guy who had gone back to being the crude dude of metal.

I never heard a word from Mason. Not even online. Using the computers at school, I tried every kind of search but never came up with the slightest lead as to what had become of him. I figured he'd get arrested again for something and his name would turn up. Or I'd read something worse. But nothing. Not a damn thing. I actually missed that sorry loser. There had been times when he had stuck up for me. Sometimes he'd been a good friend.

But life was better with him gone. He'd brought mostly trouble into my life, and probably the kindest thing he'd ever done for me was to leave me behind.

Like I say, I missed him. I really did. But now it was just me. On my own. No one to blame but me. No one to make decisions but me. For myself.

And that was hard.

I hated every minute of school. Like always. But Sean had promised to come back and "ruin" my life if I quit. A threat like that from Sean was like a bear hug, if you know what I mean.

And the story got around about me learning to play bass and hanging out with Sean Dakota. I kept working on those calluses on my fingertips. I kept practicing on the bass along with some of Sean's recorded songs. Then I started jamming with some kids from school who were also into playing music. Kids who had never talked to me before. I kept noticing that so many things were different, at school and around town. At first I didn't get it. People were treating me so differently than they had before.

And then it dawned on me.

It wasn't them who were different. It was me.

Lesley Choyce, who has been teaching English and creative writing for over thirty years, is the author of more than 100 books of literary fiction, short stories, poetry, creative nonfiction and young adult novels. He has won the Dartmouth Book Award, the Atlantic Poetry Prize and the Ann Connor Brimer Award. He has also been shortlisted for the Stephen Leacock Medal for Humour, the White Pine Award, the Hackmatack Children's Choice Book Award, the Aurora Award from the Canadian Science Fiction and Fantasy Association and, most recently, the Governor General's Literary Award. He lives at Lawrencetown Beach, Nova Scotia.

orca soundings

For more information on all the books

in the Orca Soundings line, please visit

orcabook.com